POIROT INVESTIGATES

The Jewel Robbery at the Grand Metropolitan

Agatha Christie

first published in

1924

"Poirot," I said, "a change of air would do you good."

"You think so, *mon ami*?"

"I am sure of it."

"Eh—eh?" said my friend, smiling. "It is all arranged, then?"

"You will come?"

"Where do you propose to take me?"

"Brighton. As a matter of fact, a friend of mine in the City put me on to a very good thing, and—well, I have money to burn, as the saying goes. I think a week-end at the *Grand Metropolitan* would do us all the good in the world."

"Thank you, I accept most gratefully. You

have the good heart to think of an old man. And the good heart, it is in the end worth all the little grey cells. Yes, yes, I who speak to you am in danger of forgetting that sometimes."

I did not quite relish the implication. I fancy that Poirot is sometimes a little inclined to underestimate my mental capacities. But his pleasure was so evident that I put my slight annoyance aside.

"Then, that's all right," I said hastily.

Saturday evening saw us dining at the *Grand Metropolitan* in the midst of a gay throng. All the world and his wife seemed to be at

Brighton. The dresses were marvellous, and the jewels—worn sometimes with more love of display than good taste—were something magnificent.

"*Hein*, it is a sight this!" murmured Poirot. "This is the home of the Profiteer, is it not so, Hastings?"

"Supposed to be," I replied. "But we'll hope they aren't all tarred with the Profiteering brush."

Poirot gazed round him placidly.

"The sight of so many jewels makes me wish I had turned my brains to crime, instead of to its detection. What a magnificent opportunity for some thief of distinction! Regard, Hastings, that stout woman by the pillar. She is, as you would say, plastered with gems."

I followed his eyes.

"Why," I exclaimed, "it's Mrs. Opalsen."

"You know her?"

"Slightly. Her husband is a rich stockbroker who made a fortune in the recent Oil boom."

After dinner we ran across the Opalsens in the lounge, and I introduced Poirot to them. We chatted for a few minutes, and ended by having our coffee together.

Poirot said a few words in praise of some of the costlier gems displayed on the lady's ample bosom, and she brightened up at once.

"It's a perfect hobby of mine, Mr. Poirot. I just *love* jewellery. Ed knows my weakness, and every time things go well he brings me something new. You are interested in precious stones?"

"I have had a good deal to do with

them one time and another, madame. My profession has brought me into contact with some of the most famous jewels in the world."

He went on to narrate, with discreet pseudonyms, the story of the historic jewels of a reigning house, and Mrs. Opalsen listened with bated breath.

"There now!" she exclaimed, as he ended. "If it isn't just like a play! You know, I've got some pearls of my own that have a history attached to them. I believe it's supposed to be one of the finest necklaces in the world—the pearls are so beautifully matched and so perfect in colour. I declare I really must run up and get it!"

"Oh, madame," protested Poirot, "you are too amiable. Pray do not derange yourself!"

"Oh, but I'd like to show it to you."

The buxom dame waddled across to the lift briskly

enough. Her husband, who had been talking to me, looked at Poirot inquiringly.

"Madame your wife is so amiable as to insist on showing me her pearl necklace," explained the latter.

"Oh, the pearls!" Opalsen smiled in a satisfied fashion. "Well, they *are* worth seeing. Cost a pretty penny too!

Still, the money's there all right; I could get what I paid for them any day—perhaps more. May have to, too, if things go on as they are now. Money's confoundedly tight in the City. All this infernal E.P.D." He rambled on, launching into technicalities where I could not follow him.

He was interrupted by a small page-boy who approached and murmured something in his ear.

"Eh—what? I'll come at once. Not taken ill, is she? Excuse me, gentlemen."

He left us abruptly. Poirot leaned back and lit one of his tiny Russian cigarettes. Then, carefully and meticulously, he arranged the empty coffee-cups in a neat row, and beamed happily on the result.

The minutes passed. The Opalsens did not return.

"Curious," I remarked, at length. "I wonder when they will come back."

Poirot watched the ascending spirals of

smoke, and then said thoughtfully:

"They will not come back."

"Why?"

"Because, my friend, something has happened."

"What sort of thing? How do you know?" I asked curiously.

Poirot smiled.

"A few moments ago the manager came hurriedly out of his office and ran upstairs. He was much agitated. The lift-boy is deep in talk with one of the pages. The lift-bell has rung three times, but he heeds it not. Thirdly, even the waiters are *distrait*; and to make a waiter *distrait*——" Poirot shook his head with an air of finality. "The affair must indeed be of the first magnitude. Ah, it is as I thought! Here come the police."

Two men had just entered the hotel— one in uniform, the other in plain clothes. They spoke to a page, and were immediately ushered upstairs. A few minutes later, the same boy descended and came up to where we were sitting.

"Mr. Opalsen's compliments, and would you step upstairs."

Poirot sprang nimbly to his feet. One would have said that he awaited the summons. I followed with no less alacrity.

The Opalsens' apartments were situated on the first floor. After knocking on the door, the page-boy retired, and we answered the summons, "Come in!" A strange scene met our eyes. The room was Mrs. Opalsen's bedroom, and in the centre of it, lying back in an arm-chair, was the lady herself, weeping violently.

She presented an extraordinary spectacle, with the tears making great furrows in the powder with which her complexion was liberally coated. Mr. Opalsen was striding up and down angrily. The two police officials stood in the middle of the room, one with a notebook in hand. An hotel chambermaid, looking frightened to death, stood by the fire-place; and on the other side of the room a Frenchwoman, obviously

Mrs. Opalsen's maid, was weeping and wringing her hands, with an intensity of grief that rivalled that of her mistress.

Into this pandemonium stepped Poirot,

neat and smiling. Immediately, with an energy surprising in one of her bulk, Mrs. Opalsen sprang from her chair towards him.

"There now; Ed may say what he likes, but I believe in luck, I do. It was fated I should meet you the way I did this evening, and I've a feeling that if you can't get my pearls back for me nobody can."

"Calm yourself, I pray of you, madame." Poirot patted her hand soothingly. "Reassure yourself. All will be well. Hercule Poirot will aid you!"

Mr. Opalsen turned to the police inspector.

"There will be no objection to my—er—calling in this gentleman, I suppose?"

"None at all, sir," replied the man civilly, but with complete indifference. "Perhaps now your lady's feeling better she'll just let us have the facts?"

Mrs. Opalsen looked helplessly at Poirot. He led her back to her chair.

"Seat yourself, madame, and recount to us the whole history without agitating yourself."

Thus abjured, Mrs. Opalsen dried her eyes gingerly, and began.

"I came upstairs after dinner to fetch my pearls for Mr. Poirot here to see. The chambermaid and Célestine were both in the room as usual——"

"Excuse me, madame, but what do you mean by 'as usual'?"

Mr. Opalsen explained.

"I make it a rule that no one is to come into this room unless Célestine, the maid, is there also. The chambermaid does the room in the morning while Célestine is present, and comes in after dinner to turn down the beds under the same conditions; otherwise she never enters the room."

"Well, as I was saying," continued Mrs. Opalsen, "I came up. I went to the drawer here,"— she indicated the bottom right-hand drawer of the knee-hole dressing-table—"took out my jewel-case and unlocked it. It seemed quite as usual—but the pearls were not there!"

The inspector had been busy with his notebook. "When had you last seen them?" he asked.

"They were there when I went down to dinner."

"You are sure?"

"Quite sure. I was uncertain whether to wear them or not, but in the end I decided on the emeralds, and put them back in the jewel-case."

"Who locked up the jewel-case?"

"I did. I wear the key on a chain round my neck." She held it up as she spoke.

The inspector examined it, and shrugged his shoulders.

"The thief must have had a duplicate key. No difficult matter. The lock is quite a simple one. What did you do after you'd locked the jewel-case?"

"I put it back in the bottom drawer where I always keep it."

"You didn't lock the drawer?"

"No, I never do. My maid remains in the room till I come up, so there's no need."

The inspector's face grew graver.

"Am I to understand that the jewels were there when you went down to dinner, and that since then *the maid has not left the room?*"

Suddenly, as though the horror of her own situation for the first time burst upon her, Célestine uttered a piercing shriek, and, flinging herself upon Poirot, poured out a torrent of incoherent French.

The suggestion was infamous! That she should be suspected of robbing Madame! The police were well known to be of a stupidity incredible! But Monsieur, who was a Frenchman—

"A Belgian," interjected Poirot, but Célestine paid no attention to the correction.

Monsieur would not stand by and see her falsely accused, while that infamous chambermaid was allowed to go scot-free. She had never liked her—a bold, red-faced thing—a born thief. She had said from the first that she was not honest. And had kept a sharp watch over her too, when she was doing Madame's room! Let those idiots of policemen search her, and if they did not find Madame's pearls on her it would be very surprising!

Although this harangue was uttered in rapid and virulent French, Célestine had interlarded it with a wealth of gesture, and the chambermaid realized at least a part of her meaning. She reddened angrily.

"If that foreign woman's saying I took the pearls, it's a lie!" she declared heatedly. "I never so much as saw them."

"Search her!" screamed the other. "You will find it is as I say."

"You're a liar—do you hear?" said the chambermaid, advancing upon her. "Stole 'em yourself, and want to put it on me. Why, I was only in the room about three minutes before the lady come up, and then you were sitting here the whole time, as you always do, like a cat watching a mouse."

The inspector looked across inquiringly at Célestine. "Is that true? Didn't you leave the room at all?"

"I did not actually leave her alone," admitted Célestine

reluctantly, "but I went into my own room through the door here twice— once to fetch a reel of cotton, and once for my scissors. She must have done it then."

"You wasn't gone a minute," retorted the chambermaid angrily. "Just popped out and in again. I'd be glad if the police *would* search me. I've nothing to be afraid of."

At this moment there was a tap at the door. The inspector went to it. His face brightened when he saw who it was.

"Ah!" he said. "That's rather fortunate. I sent for one of our female searchers, and she's just arrived. Perhaps if you wouldn't mind going into the room next door."

He looked at the chambermaid, who stepped across the threshold with a toss of her head, the searcher following her closely.

The French girl had sunk sobbing into a chair. Poirot was looking round the room, the main features of which I have made clear by a sketch.

[A sketch of the bedroom, adjoining maid's room, and corridor.]

"Where does that door lead?" he inquired, nodding his head towards the one by the window.

"Into the next apartment, I believe,"

said the inspector. "It's bolted, anyway, on this side."

Poirot walked across to it, tried it, then drew back the bolt and tried it again.

"And on the other side as well," he remarked. "Well, that seems to rule out that."

He walked over to the windows,

examining each of them in turn.

"And again—nothing. Not even a balcony outside."

"Even if there were," said the inspector impatiently, "I don't see how that would help us, if the maid never left the room."

"Évidemment," said Poirot, not disconcerted. "As

Mademoiselle is positive she did not leave the room——"

He was interrupted by the reappearance of the chambermaid and the police searcher.

"Nothing," said the latter laconically.

"I should hope not, indeed," said the chambermaid virtuously. "And that

French hussy ought to be ashamed of herself taking away an honest girl's character!"

"There, there, my girl; that's all right," said the inspector, opening the door. "Nobody suspects you. You go along and get on with your work."

The chambermaid went unwillingly.

"Going to search *her*?" she demanded, pointing at Célestine.

"Yes, yes!" He shut the door on her and turned the key.

Célestine accompanied the searcher into the small room in her turn. A few minutes later she also returned. Nothing had been found on her.

The inspector's face grew graver.

"I'm afraid I'll have to ask you to come along with me all the same, miss." He turned to Mrs. Opalsen. "I'm sorry, madam, but all the evidence points that way. If she's not got them on her, they're hidden somewhere about the room."

Célestine uttered a piercing shriek, and clung to Poirot's arm. The latter bent and whispered something in the girl's ear. She looked up at him doubtfully.

"*Si, si, mon enfant*—I assure you it is better not to resist." Then he turned to the inspector. "You permit, monsieur? A little experiment—purely for my own satisfaction."

"Depends on what it is," replied the police officer non-committally.

Poirot addressed Célestine once more.

"You have told us that you went into your room to fetch a reel of cotton. Whereabouts was it?"

"On the top of the chest of drawers, monsieur."

"And the scissors?"

"They also."

"Would it be troubling you too much, mademoiselle, to ask you to repeat those two actions? You were sitting here with your work, you say?"

Célestine sat down, and then, at a sign from Poirot, rose, passed into the adjoining room, took up an object from the chest of drawers, and returned.

Poirot divided his attention between her movements and a large turnip of a watch which he held in the palm of his hand.

"Again, if you please, mademoiselle."

At the conclusion of the second performance, he made a note in his pocket-book, and returned the watch to his pocket.

"Thank you, mademoiselle. And you, monsieur,"— he bowed to the inspector—"for your courtesy."

The inspector seemed somewhat entertained by this excessive politeness. Célestine departed in a flood of tears, accompanied by the woman and the plain-clothes official.

Then, with a brief apology to Mrs. Opalsen, the inspector set to work to ransack the room. He pulled out drawers, opened cupboards, completely unmade the bed, and tapped the floor. Mr. Opalsen looked on sceptically.

"You really think you will find them?"

"Yes, sir. It stands to reason. She hadn't time to take them out of the room. The lady's discovering the robbery so soon upset her plans. No, they're here right enough. One of the two must have hidden them—and it's very unlikely for the chambermaid to have done so."

"More than unlikely—impossible!" said Poirot quietly.

"Eh?" The inspector stared.

Poirot smiled modestly.

"I will demonstrate. Hastings, my good friend, take my watch in your hand—with care. It is a family heirloom! Just now I timed Mademoiselle's movements—her first absence from the room was of twelve seconds, her second of fifteen. Now observe my actions. Madame will have the kindness to give me the key of the jewel-case. I thank you. My friend Hastings will have the kindness to say 'Go!'"

"Go!" I said.

With almost incredible swiftness, Poirot wrenched open the drawer of the dressing-table, extracted the jewel-case, fitted the key in the lock, opened the case, selected a piece of jewellery, shut and locked the case, and returned it to the drawer, which he pushed to again. His movements were like lightning.

"Well, *mon ami*?" he demanded of me breathlessly.

"Forty-six seconds," I replied.

"You see?" He looked round. "There would not have been time for the chambermaid even to take the necklace out, far less hide it."

"Then that settles it on the maid," said the inspector with satisfaction, and returned to his search. He passed into the maid's bedroom next door.

Poirot was frowning thoughtfully. Suddenly he shot a question at Mr. Opalsen.

"This necklace—it was, without doubt, insured?"

Mr. Opalsen looked a trifle surprised at the question.

"Yes," he said hesitatingly, "that is so."

"But what does that matter?" broke in Mrs. Opalsen tearfully. "It's my necklace I want. It was unique. No money could be the same."

"I comprehend, madame," said Poirot soothingly. "I comprehend perfectly. To *la femme* sentiment is everything—is it not so? But monsieur, who has not the so fine susceptibility, will doubtless find some slight consolation in the fact."

"Of course, of course," said Mr. Opalsen rather uncertainly. "Still——"

He was interrupted by a shout of triumph from the inspector. He came in dangling something from his fingers.

With a cry, Mrs. Opalsen heaved herself up from her chair. She was a changed woman.

"Oh, oh, my necklace!"

She clasped it to her breast with both hands. We crowded round.

"Where was it?" demanded Opalsen.

"Maid's bed. In among the springs of the wire mattress. She must have stolen it and hidden it there before the chambermaid arrived on the scene."

"You permit, madame?" said Poirot gently. He took the necklace from her and examined it closely; then handed it back with a bow.

"I'm afraid, madam, you'll have to hand it over to us for the time being," said the inspector. "We shall want it for the charge. But it shall be returned to you as soon as possible."

Mr. Opalsen frowned.

"Is that necessary?"

"I'm afraid so, sir. Just a formality."

"Oh, let him take it, Ed!" cried his wife. "I'd feel safer if he did. I shouldn't sleep a wink thinking some one else might try and get hold of it.

That wretched girl! And I would never have believed it of her."

"There, there, my dear, don't take on so."

I felt a gentle pressure on my arm. It was Poirot.

"Shall we slip away, my friend? I think our services are no longer needed."

Once outside, however, he hesitated, and then, much to my surprise, he remarked:

"I should rather like to see the room next door."

The door was not locked, and we entered. The room, which was a large double one, was unoccupied. Dust lay about rather noticeably, and my sensitive friend gave a characteristic grimace as he ran his finger round a rectangular mark on a table near the window.

"The *service* leaves to be desired," he observed dryly.

He was staring thoughtfully out of the window, and seemed to have fallen into a brown study.

"Well?" I demanded impatiently. "What did we come in here for?"

He started.

"*Je vous demande pardon, mon ami.* I wished to see if the door was really bolted on this side also."

"Well," I said, glancing at the door which communicated with the room we had just left, "it *is* bolted."

Poirot nodded. He still seemed to be thinking.

"And, anyway," I continued, "what does it matter? The case is over. I wish you'd had more chance of distinguishing yourself. But it was the kind of case that even a stiff-backed idiot like that inspector couldn't go wrong over."

Poirot shook his head.

"The case is not over, my friend. It will not be over until we find out who stole the pearls."

"But the maid did!"

"Why do you say that?"

"Why," I stammered, "they were found—actually in her mattress."

"Ta, ta, ta!" said Poirot impatiently. "Those were not the pearls."

"What?"

"Imitation, *mon ami*."

The statement took my breath away. Poirot was smiling placidly.

"The good inspector obviously knows nothing of jewels. But presently there will be a fine hullabaloo!"

"Come!" I cried, dragging at his arm.

"Where?"

"We must tell the Opalsens at once."

"I think not."

"But that poor woman——"

"*Eh bien*; that poor woman, as you call her, will have a much better night believing the jewels to be safe."

"But the thief may escape with them!"

"As usual, my friend, you speak without reflection. How do you know that the pearls Mrs. Opalsen locked up so carefully to-night were not the false ones, and that the real robbery did not take place at a much earlier date?"

"Oh!" I said, bewildered.

"Exactly," said Poirot, beaming. "We start again."

He led the way out of the room, paused a moment as though considering, and then walked down to the end of the corridor, stopping outside the small den where the chambermaids and valets of the respective floors congregated.

Our particular chambermaid appeared to be holding a small court there, and to be retailing her late experiences to an appreciative audience. She stopped in the middle of a sentence. Poirot bowed with his usual politeness.

"Excuse that I derange you, but

I shall be obliged if you will unlock for me the door of Mr. Opalsen's room."

The woman rose willingly, and we accompanied her down the passage again. Mr. Opalsen's room was on the other side of the corridor, its door facing that of his wife's room. The chambermaid unlocked it with her pass-key, and we entered.

As she was about to depart Poirot detained her.

"One moment; have you ever seen among the effects of Mr. Opalsen a card like this?"

He held out a plain white card, rather highly glazed

and uncommon in appearance. The maid took it and scrutinized it carefully.

"No, sir, I can't say I have. But, anyway, the valet has most to do with the gentlemen's rooms."

"I see. Thank you."

Poirot took back the card. The woman departed. Poirot

appeared to reflect a little. Then he gave a short, sharp nod of the head.

"Ring the bell, I pray of you, Hastings. Three times, for the valet."

I obeyed, devoured with curiosity. Meanwhile Poirot had emptied the waste-paper-basket on the floor, and was swiftly going through its contents.

In a few moments the valet answered the bell. To him Poirot put the same question, and handed him the card to examine. But the response was the same. The valet had never seen a card of that particular quality among Mr. Opalsen's belongings. Poirot thanked him, and he withdrew, somewhat unwillingly, with an inquisitive glance at the overturned waste-paper-basket and the litter on the floor. He could hardly have helped overhearing Poirot's thoughtful remark as he bundled the torn papers back again:

"And the necklace was heavily insured. . . ."

"Poirot," I cried, "I see——"

"You see nothing, my friend," he replied quickly. "As usual, nothing at all! It is incredible—but there it is. Let us return to our own apartments."

We did so in silence. Once there, to my

intense surprise, Poirot effected a rapid change of clothing.

"I go to London to-night," he explained. "It is imperative."

"What?"

"Absolutely. The real work, that of the brain (ah, those brave little grey cells), it is done. I go to seek

the confirmation.
I shall find it!
Impossible to deceive
Hercule Poirot!"

"You'll come a
cropper one of these
days," I observed,
rather disgusted by
his vanity.

"Do not be enraged, I
beg of you, *mon ami.*
I count on you to
do me a service—of
your friendship."

"Of course," I said eagerly, rather ashamed of my moroseness. "What is it?"

"The sleeve of my coat that I have taken off—will you brush it? See you, a little white powder has clung to it. You without doubt observed me run my finger round the drawer of the dressing-table?"

"No, I didn't."

"You should observe my actions, my friend. Thus I obtained the powder on my finger, and, being a little over-excited, I rubbed it on my sleeve; an action without method which I deplore—false to all my principles."

"But what was the powder?" I asked, not particularly interested in Poirot's principles.

"Not the poison of the Borgias," replied Poirot, with a twinkle. "I see your imagination mounting. I should say it was French chalk."

"French chalk?"

"Yes, cabinet-makers use it to make drawers run smoothly."

I laughed.

"You old sinner! I thought you were working up to something exciting."

"Au revoir, my friend. I save myself. I fly!"

The door shut behind him. With a smile,

half of derision, half of affection, I picked up the coat, and stretched out my hand for the clothes-brush.

• • • • • • •

The next morning, hearing nothing from Poirot, I went out for a stroll, met some old friends, and lunched with them at their hotel. In the afternoon we went for a spin. A punctured tyre delayed us, and it was past eight when I got back to the *Grand Metropolitan*.

The first sight that met my eyes was Poirot, looking even more diminutive than usual, sandwiched between the Opalsens, beaming in a state of placid satisfaction.

"*Mon ami* Hastings!" he cried, and sprang to meet me. "Embrace me, my friend; all has marched to a marvel!"

Luckily, the embrace was merely figurative—not a thing one is always sure of with Poirot.

"Do you mean——" I began.

"Just wonderful, I call it!" said Mrs. Opalsen, smiling all over her fat face. "Didn't I tell you, Ed, that if he couldn't get back my pearls nobody would?"

"You did, my dear, you did. And you were right."

I looked helplessly at Poirot, and he answered the glance.

"My friend Hastings is, as you say in England, all at the seaside. Seat yourself, and I will recount to you all the affair that has so happily ended."

"Ended?"

"But yes. They are arrested."

"Who are arrested?"

"The chambermaid and the valet, *parbleu!* You did not suspect? Not with my parting hint about the French chalk?"

"You said cabinet-makers used it."

"Certainly they do—to make drawers slide easily. Somebody wanted that drawer to slide in and out without any noise.

Who could that be? Obviously, only the chambermaid. The plan was so ingenious that it did not at once leap to the eye—not even to the eye of Hercule Poirot.

"Listen, this was how it was done. The valet was in the empty room next door, waiting. The French maid leaves the room.

Quick as a flash the chambermaid whips open the drawer, takes out the jewel-case, and, slipping back the bolt, passes it through the door. The valet opens it at his leisure with the duplicate key with which he has provided himself, extracts the necklace, and waits his time. Célestine leaves the room again, and—pst!—in a flash the case is passed back again and replaced in the drawer.

"Madame arrives, the theft is discovered. The chambermaid demands to be searched, with a good deal of righteous indignation, and leaves the room without a stain on her character. The imitation necklace with which they have provided themselves has been concealed in the French girl's bed that morning by the chambermaid—a master stroke, ça!"

"But what did you go to London for?"

"You remember the card?"

"Certainly. It puzzled me—and puzzles me still. I thought——"

I hesitated delicately, glancing at Mr. Opalsen.

Poirot laughed heartily.

"*Une blague!* For the benefit of the valet. The card was one with a specially prepared surface—for finger-prints. I went straight to Scotland Yard, asked for our old friend Inspector Japp, and laid the facts before him. As I had suspected, the finger-prints proved to be those of two well-known jewel thieves who have been 'wanted' for some time. Japp came down with me, the thieves were arrested, and the necklace was discovered in the valet's possession. A clever pair, but they failed in *method*. Have I not told you, Hastings, at least thirty-six times, that without method——"

"At least thirty-six thousand times!" I interrupted. "But where did their 'method' break down?"

"*Mon ami*, it is a good plan to take a place as chambermaid or valet—but you must not shirk your work. They left an empty room undusted; and therefore, when the man put down the jewel-case on the little table near the communicating door, it left a square mark——"

"I remember," I cried.

"Before, I was undecided. Then—I *knew!*" There was a moment's silence.

"And I've got my pearls," said Mrs. Opalsen as a sort of Greek chorus.

"Well," I said, "I'd better have some dinner." Poirot accompanied me.

"This ought to mean kudos for you," I observed.

"*Pas du tout*," replied Poirot tranquilly. "Japp and the local inspector will divide the credit between them. But"—he tapped his pocket—"I have a cheque here, from Mr. Opalsen, and, how say you, my friend? This week-end has not gone according to plan. Shall we return here next week-end— at my expense this time?"

ABOUT THE AUTHOR

Agatha Christie's wrote her first novel while working as a nurse in World War I. But it would take four years, six rejections, and an American publisher before the world would meet Hercule Poirot. Now her books have sold over 2 billion copies and been translated into 103 languages. Her play "The Mousetrap" has run continuously since 1952, setting another record. Poirot and her other most famous detective, Miss Marple live on in countless film and tv adaptations. In 1971, she was appointed a Dame Commander of the Order of the British Empire (DBE). She died five years later at the age of 85.

WHAT WE'RE ABOUT

I made the first Super Large Print books for my grandma. She needed books she could keep reading as her glaucoma and macular degeneration advanced. I used a font originally made for people with dyslexia, because the letters are bold and easy to distinguish. The books are set at 30 pt font, twice the size of traditional Large Print. Being able to read again was life changing.

Digital reading was too frustrating for my grandma. And it could never offer the pleasures she had always associated with reading. The peaceful rhythm of turning a page. The satisfaction in knowing a story has "this much left". And the comforting memories of adventure, companionship, and revelation she felt when seeing the cover of her favorite book. Part of what makes reading so relaxing and grounding is the tactile experience. I hope these books can bring joy to those who want to keep reading and to those who've never had the pleasure of curling up with a page turner.

Please let me know if you have any requests for new titles. To leave feedback and to see the complete and constantly updating catalog, please visit:

superlargeprint.com

MORE BOOKS AT:

superlargeprint.com

KEEP ON READING!

ISBN 9798716921313

Made in the USA
Middletown, DE
20 December 2023

46450359R00070